MARY LENNOX was a grumpy, straggly-haired, thin child with a permanent scowl on her face. But then, she'd had a strange upbringing.

She had been brought up by servants in India, until a dreadful fever swept through the house. Within days, everyone Mary knew had been lost to the illness, so she was sent across the seas to live with her uncle, Archibald Craven, in a place called Yorkshire, in England.

Yorkshire was a very, very long way away from India.

After weeks at sea, Mary arrived in London and was met by a stern-faced woman called Mrs Medlock – her uncle's housekeeper.

The wind howled and the rain lashed down as they drew closer to Mary's new home, Misselthwaite Manor, high on the bleak, dark moors.

The Secret Garden

RETOLD BY
Claire Freedman

ILLUSTRATED BY
Shaw Davidson

PUFFIN BOOKS

UK | USA | Canada | Ireland | Australia
India | New Zealand | South Africa

Puffin Books is part of the Penguin Random House group of companies
whose addresses can be found at global.penguinrandomhouse.com.

www.penguin.co.uk www.puffin.co.uk www.ladybird.co.uk

First published 2020
001

Printed in China

A CIP catalogue record for this book is available from the British Library

ISBN: 978-0-241-39278-2

All correspondence to: Puffin Books, One Embassy Gardens, New Union Square,
5 Nine Elms Lane, London SW8 5DA

"I don't like this place," Mary said, pinching her thin lips. "Will my uncle be there to meet me?"

"Mr Craven is away travelling," Mrs Medlock said. "You're to keep out of everyone's way while he's gone."

On Mary's first morning in the manor, she was woken by a young maid.

"Are you here to wash and dress me?" Mary asked.

"Goodness me – no!" exclaimed the maid, whose name was Martha. "You're big enough to dress yourself!"

Mary scowled as she got ready. She had no appetite for breakfast.

“I don’t like it here,” she said. “What shall I do all day?”

“My brother Dickon loves to run on the moors,” Martha said. “He spends hours out there, and makes friends with the birds and other animals. But why don’t you explore the gardens first? There’s lots to see.”

“I suppose so,” said Mary.

Dressed warmly, Mary began to explore the gardens. It was winter, so the flower beds were bare and the fountain was shut off. Frosty leaves scrunched underfoot, and the cold air stung her face.

Mary wandered aimlessly through many gardens, which all looked much the same to her. But then she stumbled upon a walled garden which seemed to have no door at all.

"How odd!" Mary thought, interested in spite of herself. She walked all the way round, searching for a way in but found nothing.

She could see tall trees peeking out above the wall and spotted a bright-eyed bird perched on top of one of the branches.

Then Mary noticed the gardener, Ben Weatherstaff, digging nearby.

"You must be Mr Craven's niece – Mary, isn't it?" the old man said, looking up.

"Yes," Mary nodded. "I've been walking around the gardens. I saw a red-breasted bird in one of them."

To Mary's surprise, Ben whistled and the bird appeared as if out of nowhere.

"He's a robin!" Ben said. "I've known him since he was a fledging and we've been friends ever since."

"I wish I had a friend," Mary said. She suddenly felt more lonely than ever, and her face closed up into its familiar scowl.

Over the next few days, Mary spent more and more time exploring the frost-covered gardens.

She soon got to know her way around.

Each day Mary went to the wall of the garden with no door.

Often the robin was there, chirping happily at her. When she saw him, Mary couldn't help but smile.

"You've found your way inside the secret garden!" Mary called. Every day she slowly walked all the way round the mysterious wall, looking for a hidden door – but there was nothing!

One evening, at supper time, Mary couldn't contain her curiosity any longer!

"Please tell me about the secret walled garden without a door!" she begged Martha. So Martha told her the story.

"It was Mrs Craven's garden," Martha began. "Mr Craven had it made especially for her, and she loved it. But one day as she was sitting high up in a tree, a branch broke and she fell to the ground, badly hurt. The next day she died, and Mr Craven was so heartbroken he locked the door, and buried the key so no one could go in! That was ten years ago!"

"That's so sad," Mary said. Then suddenly, in the distance, she heard the sound of someone crying. "Listen! Do you hear that?"

Martha looked flustered all of a sudden.

"It's probably just the wind whistling," she said.

In the distance a door slammed, and then the house fell back into silence.

"No more stories, young lady," said Martha briskly. "It's time for bed!"

The next day it was raining. There could be no going outside.

"You haven't even begun to explore the house yet!" Martha smiled. "It's the perfect day to have a good look around."

So Mary set off down one of the long corridors of the manor.

There were many, many rooms, leading off from each side.
Mary peeked into them all,
but each one was empty.

Just then the stillness
was broken by a cry!

"There *is* someone crying!" Mary said. She was determined to investigate, but as she hurried towards the sound, she ran straight into Mrs Medlock.

"I heard someone crying!" Mary told the housekeeper.

"Nonsense!" Mrs Medlock said. "Come along now!" And she roughly took Mary back down the corridor to her own room.

Two days later the rain stopped and the sun came out. Mary was happy to be able to play outside again, and even happier when the robin flew down to join her.

"You remember me!" she cried. "You do!" She watched as the robin hopped about over some freshly turned-up earth. Mary looked down. There was something in the ground like a ring of iron. Mary tugged and tugged and suddenly the ring came free.

"It's a key!" she gasped.
"Perhaps it has been buried for ten years . . .
Perhaps it is the key to the secret garden!"

At the very moment that thought occurred to her, the robin flew up from the ground in a gust of wind that blew aside some loose ivy trails.

And Mary spotted it – a round knob – the knob of a door!

The robin twittered excitedly as Mary pushed away the ivy.

It was a door

with a lock

and the key fitted!

Mary pushed

and slowly

the door opened.

Breathless with wonder, Mary was standing inside the secret garden!
It was the most mysterious garden anyone could ever imagine.
There were hazy tangles of vines hanging between the trees.

Were they still alive?

The robin hopped from bush to bush
as if showing her things.
Everything was strange and silent.
There were tiny green shoots
growing from the dark
earthy borders.

"Yes it is alive!" Mary whispered. "But it needs tending!" She bent down and started to clear a little patch to help the shoots breathe until it was time to go back to the house for lunch.

Mary wanted to keep the garden her secret.

She spent a week in the pale winter sunshine, tidying it as best she could with her bare hands.

She found lots of bulbs and tiny green shoots. What would they become?

One evening she said carefully to Martha, "I wish I had a little spade so I could make a garden of my own."

Martha smiled. "Leave it with me," she said.

The next day, as Mary walked towards the garden, she saw a boy.

"Don't move!" he whispered.

As he stood, Mary saw a squirrel and a rabbit scamper away from him, and her face broke into a smile.

"I know who you are," she said. "You're Martha's brother, Dickon!"

The boy smiled too. "And you're Mary, aren't you? Martha mentioned you asked for some tools. I've brought you a spade and fork and trowel and some seeds. I can help you plant them. Where's your garden?"

Mary liked Dickon immediately.

"Can you keep a secret?" she asked.

"I keep secrets all the time," Dickon replied. "Secrets about fox cubs and birds' nests!"

So Mary led Dickon to her secret garden.

Dickon stared around him in awe. "There's lots of dead wood to be cut off," he said, going round with his knife cutting off branches. He kneeled and cut off some lifeless twigs. "See," he said, "there's green below!"

"Could we bring the garden back to life?" Mary said.

"I reckon!" Dickon replied. "There's lots of work to be done but I can help you."

"You won't tell anyone?" Mary asked.

"Never!" laughed Dickon.

That night, Mary woke up to the sound of crying.

"I'm going to find out what it is," she decided.

The faint, far-off crying led her down the long dark corridors to a door.

Mary pushed it open and stepped inside.

At the end of the gloomy room was a huge bed, and in it was a boy of her own age, his face wet with tears.

"Are you a ghost?" the boy said.

"No!" Mary answered. "Who are you? Why are you crying?"

"My name is Colin," sobbed the boy. "I'm very ill and I'm frightened I might never be well again."

"Oh!" said Mary, feeling sorry for the boy.

So she told him stories about robins, flowers and a secret garden until he fell asleep.

The next morning the moor was hidden in a white mist and the rain was pouring down. In fact, it stayed rainy all week. But Mary wasn't bored. She spent her days with Colin.

She learned that his father was Mr Craven.

"Then you're my cousin!" she gasped, amazed to have found some family at last. "Tell me about your father," she said.

"I hardly see him," replied Colin sadly. "I don't think he can bear to look at me. My mother died when I was a baby and I've always been ill. My doctor and nurses say I won't live long."

Colin began to cry again, but Mary found she could cheer him up by talking.

They talked about everything – the moor, Dickon, the robin and his nest, and especially the secret garden – though Mary didn't share that she had been inside. In fact, Mary talked more than she had ever done before, and Colin both talked and listened as *he* had never done either. They laughed and laughed together like good friends, and Colin quite forgot he was a sickly boy! In fact, Mary wondered if he had ever been as ill as people thought.

After days of endless rain, one morning Mary woke up to brilliant sunshine.

"I'll be able to go outside today!" she cried excitedly.

So instead of visiting Colin as usual, she dashed out. She couldn't wait to get to the secret garden.

Dickon was already there, hard at work. A little bushy-tailed fox sat beside him, and a rook flew down from a branch and settled on his shoulder. The robin was busily building his nest.

"Come and see!" Dickon said. He showed Mary a clump of purple and yellow crocuses that had burst through, and a thousand tiny green shoots.

"Do you know about Colin?" Mary asked Dickon, as they worked on the garden together.

"He's the poorly lad who can't walk," Dickon replied.

"I've been thinking . . ." said Mary. "If we took Colin out here, the fresh air might make him better. It has helped me."

"Aye!" nodded Dickon.

After saying goodbye to Dickon, Mary couldn't wait to tell Colin their plan. She ran back to the house as fast as she could, and raced up to his room.

But Colin was in a terrible mood!

"How dare you play with Dickon and not see me!" he sulked.

All at once, Mary's excitement vanished and she stamped her foot in anger.

"I'll do what I like," she said. "And I don't believe you are ill – you just want people to feel sorry for you!"

Colin was so angry he threw
a cushion at Mary in a not-very-sick way!

"I'm going and I'm not coming back!" shouted Mary.

That night, Mary woke to the sound of loud wailing.

"It's Colin!" panicked Martha, bursting into her room. "His nurses say he's having hysterics."

"I'll go to him," Mary said.

Colin was crying wildly. "I'm so ill I'm probably dying!" he shrieked.

"Stop it!" Mary said. "I'm sure you are not as ill as you think you are! I think you could even come outside if you really wanted to!"

"Really?" said Colin, slumping down in relief.

"Yes!" replied Mary, feeling her anger at Colin melting away. "And I have something exciting to tell you. I've found the key to the secret garden and been inside with Dickon!"

"Oh, Mary!" Colin cried. "Will I live to see inside it myself?"

"Of course you will," Mary smiled, "and if you get dressed and out of bed this afternoon, Dickon will come to see you - and bring his animals with him!"

And that's just what happened.

Dickon came with a fox, the crow, and a squirrel and a lamb, and spoke about the blue sky and green earth and flowers bursting forth and springtime. Just talking and laughing made Colin feel stronger.

His doctors and nurses were amazed.

Things were changing in the manor!

Everyone came together to prepare Colin for the big day. His nurse dressed him warmly, the strongest footman carried him downstairs, put him in his wheeled chair, and arranged his blankets and cushions.

Dickon pushed the chair slowly and Colin raised his face towards the sun, breathing in the soft, fresh air. "What is that scent?" Colin cried.

"It's the gorse on the moor," Dickon said.

They weaved in and out
of the shrubbery.

"This is where the robin
flew over the wall!"
breathed Mary.

"And this – this is the door to the secret garden," Dickon said, pushing Colin inside. The sun fell on Colin's face, the bees hummed, the birds chirped and the sweet-smelling crocuses bloomed gold, purple and white.

"I shall get well! I shall get well!"
cried Colin, feeling the magic already.

Dickon wheeled Colin all around the garden, pointing out different trees and creatures and green shoots.

"Do you think we'll see the robin?" Colin asked.

"He's busy patching up his nest with twigs," Dickon said. "Look, there he goes!"

Colin laughed. His normally pale cheeks were pink.

“We’ll have you digging and walking here soon!” Dickon smiled.

“Walk!” gasped Colin. “Shall I?”

“Of course!” Mary said happily, her own face glowing.

“Look!” cried Colin suddenly.

Over the top of the wall they could see the cross face of the gardener, Ben Weatherstaff, glaring at them.

"How did you get in?" he asked angrily. "You have no right to be in here!"

Just then Ben caught sight of Colin in his wheeled chair. His jaw dropped.

"Do you know who I am?" Colin asked the old man.

"Aye – I do!" Ben gulped. "You are that poor boy who can't walk!"

“I can walk!” said Colin indignantly, and, saying those words, a sudden strength ran through him.

“He can do it, he can do it!” Mary repeated

The rugs and cushions were tossed aside. Dickon held Colin’s arms and suddenly Colin was standing up, as straight as could be!

To Mary’s surprise, tears ran down Ben Weatherstaff’s sun-worn, wrinkled face.

“Eh, lad!” he said. “There’s naught wrong with your legs. God bless thee!”

“Now you’ve seen us, you must keep the garden a secret!” Colin said.

“Aye!” the old man replied. “That I will!”

As the garden blossomed, so did Colin and Mary.

They spent each day outside, gardening and Mary helping Colin to learn to walk.

After barely eating for years, suddenly Colin was forever hungry. Mary grew happier and healthier as the garden worked its magic on her too.

"What happens in the garden must be our secret!" Colin told Mary. "No one must know I am getting better until I can run and walk! Then I can surprise my father when he comes home!"

Back at the house, the doctor and nurses noticed a change in Colin, but they had no idea just how improved he really was. Beyond the garden he pretended he was still ill.

Meanwhile, Colin's father, Archibald Craven, was away travelling, when he suddenly felt a strong urge to come home.

Maybe the magic of the garden was calling him.

When Archibald arrived home, the first thing he did was summon Colin's doctor.

"Colin seems to be getting better," the doctor said. "But we're not quite sure why. He is out in the gardens! He's always in the gardens!"

"The gardens?" gasped Mr Craven. Deep down, a memory stirred of a garden bursting with flowers and green leaves, and a young woman laughing with joy. But that garden had been shut up for years.

Colin led his father into the garden.

It was ablaze, a riot of colour. On every side the flowers blossomed brightly, and the scent of roses and lavender filled the air.

"I thought the garden would be dead," Colin's father gasped.

Mr Craven walked outside, past the fountain and leafy trees. He felt as if he were being pulled, pulled to the secret garden. He could hear the joyful sounds of children playing, and he followed the sounds of laughter until he reached the wall of the garden he had shut up ten years ago.

"I must be dreaming!" he cried.
"Surely the garden is locked up –
I buried the key!"

Suddenly the door burst open
and out rushed a boy.
A tall, handsome boy.
A boy full of life and happiness.

"Father!" cried Colin. "It's me! It really is!"
"You're well!" Mr Craven cried with joy, as he hugged his son.

“I thought so too!” Mary smiled. “But it’s come alive!”

Then Colin told his father the story – a wonderful story about Mary coming to Yorkshire, and befriending the robin . . . about finding the key to the garden . . . about Dickon and his animals . . . and, most of all, about the magic of the secret garden.

“Now,” Colin said, “the garden need not be a secret any more.”

And as the sun set crimson red, they all walked
back to the manor, side by side.
The house staff stared in wonder – it was like a miracle.
Their old master looked happy and carefree,
and his son walked tall, with his head held high –
like any other boy touched by magic.